The Fox and the Crow

RETOLD AND ILLUSTRATED BY GRAHAM PERCY

For Lucie

Distributed in the United States of America by
The Child's World®
1980 Lookout Drive • Mankato, MN 56003-1705
800-599-READ • www.childsworld.com

ACKNOWLEDGMENTS
The Child's World®: Mary Berendes, Publishing Director
The Design Lab: Kathleen Petelinsek, Art Direction and Design;
Anna Petelinsek, Page Production

COPYRIGHT

LIBRARY OF CONGRESS CATALOGING-IN-PUBLICATION DATA
Percy, Graham.
  The fox and the crow / retold and illustrated by Graham Percy.
    p. cm. — (Aesop's fables)
  Summary: A fox plays upon a crow's vanity to steal a piece of cheese.
  ISBN 978-1-60253-199-4 (lib. bound : alk. paper)
  [1. Fables. 2. Folklore.] I. Aesop. II. Title. III. Series.
  PZ8.2.P435Fo 2009
  398.2—dc22
  [E]   2009001583

Those who compliment you might only be seeking something for themselves.

Once there was a big, black crow. He thought he was better than everyone else. He was very proud of himself. He strutted around, showing off to all the other animals.

"What a very fine crow I am!" he would say. He loved to see his shadow on the ground and his reflection in the water.

One day, the crow passed a small farmhouse with an open door. Being a nosy bird, he wanted to see inside. He hopped right through the door and into the kitchen.

The farmer and his wife had left bits of their lunch on the table. There was bread, butter, milk, and . . . cheese.

"Yum!" said the crow. "Cheese is my favorite!"

The crow picked up a big chunk of cheese in his beak. He flapped out the door and flew to a nearby tree.

The crow did not know it,
but he was being watched.
Hidden in the garden, a hungry
fox licked his lips.

The fox wanted the cheese for himself.

"I know the crow won't share it with me," he thought, "and I can't climb the tree and grab it from him. How can I get the cheese?"

The fox thought and thought.
Then he had an idea. He walked
over to the tree and called up to
the crow.

"Hello, Mr. Crow! I'm so glad to meet such a fine fellow as you. How beautiful you are with your mighty wings and your shiny feathers. I've heard you can sing, too! Would you please sing for me?"

The proud crow loved
hearing compliments such as
these. He couldn't help himself.
He stretched his neck and
ruffled his feathers. He shuffled
along the branch and got ready
to sing for the fox.

He opened his mouth to
sing . . . and out fell the cheese!

The smart fox was waiting below, and caught the cheese in his mouth. He happily gobbled it all up.

The crow watched sadly as the last bits of cheese went down the fox's throat. He had been outsmarted!

Two sparrows had been watching everything from the garden gate.

One chirped wisely to the other, "You can't always trust those who compliment you. They might only be seeking something for themselves."

AESOP

Aesop was a storyteller who lived more than 2,500 years ago. He lived so long ago, there isn't much information about him. Most people believe Aesop was a slave who lived in the area around the Mediterranean Sea—probably in or near the country of Greece.

Aesop's fables are known in almost every culture in the world, in almost every language. His fables are even *part* of some languages! Some common phrases come from Aesop's fables, such as "sour grapes" and "Don't count your chickens before they're hatched."

ABOUT FABLES

Fables are one of the oldest forms of stories. They are often short and funny, and have animals as the main characters. These animals act like people. Often, fables teach the reader a lesson. This is called a *moral*. A moral might teach right from wrong, or show how to act in good, kind ways. A moral might show what happens when someone makes a poor decision. Fables teach us how to live wisely.

ABOUT THE ILLUSTRATOR

Graham Percy was a famous illustrator of more than one hundred books. He was born and raised in New Zealand. He first studied art at the Elam School of Art in New Zealand and then moved to London, England, to study at the Royal College of Art.

Mr. Percy especially loved to draw animals, many types of which can be found in his books. He illustrated books on everything from mysteries to lullabies. He was even a designer for the animated film "Hugo the Hippo." Mr. Percy lived most of his life in London.